KT-425-927

ELGIN

lauren child

PUFFIN

Text based on script written by Bridget Hurst and Carol Noble

Illustrations from the TV animation produced by Tiger Aspect

With special thanks to Leigh Hodgkinson

PUFFIN BOOKS
Published by the Penguin Group: London, New York, Ireland, Australia,
Canada, India, New Zealand and South Africa
Penguin Books Ltd, Registered Offices: 80 Strand, London WC2R 0RL, England

www.penguin.com

First published 2005
7 9 10 8 6

Made and printed in China
ISBN-13: 978-0-141-38211-1
ISBN-10: 0-141-38211-2

I have this little sister Lola.
She is small and very funny.
Lola loves reading and she really loves books.
But at the moment there is
one book that is extra specially special.

One day, Lola said,

"Charlie, Dad says he will take us to the library and we must go right now and get Beetles, Bugs and Butterflies."

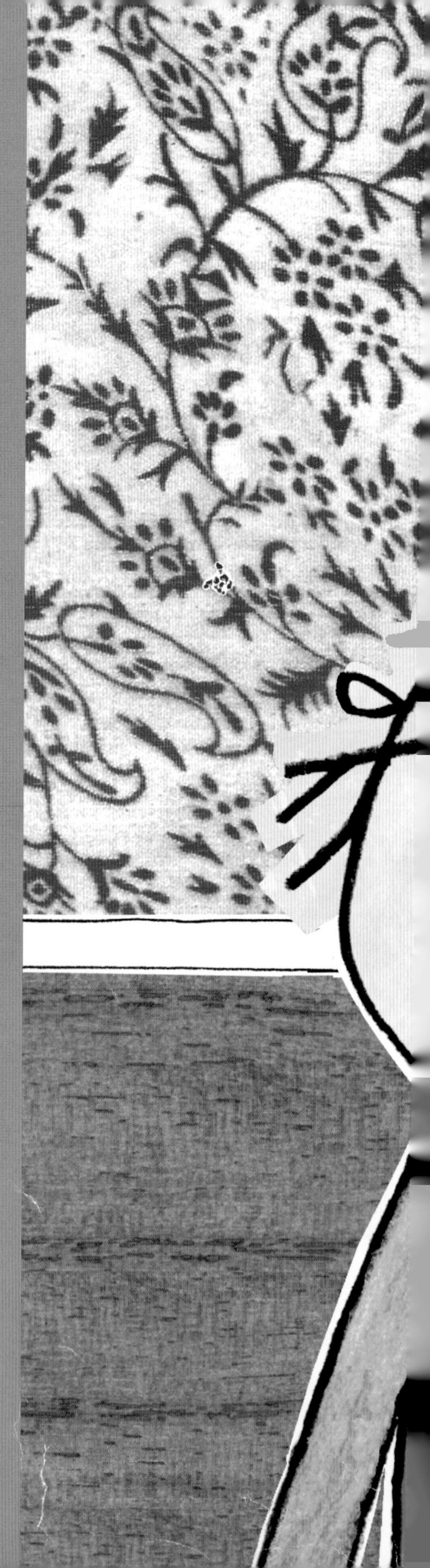

Lola loves Beetles, Bugs and Butterflies.

I say,

"But Dad took that book out for you last time...
And the time before that..."

Then Lola says,
"But Charlie, Beetles, Bugs and Butterflies is a very special book that is my favourite and I really need it.

Now.

Now.

Now.

Now.

Now!

Don't you know Beetles, Bugs and Butterflies is the best book in the whole world?"

And Lola says,

"You see, Charlie,

the bugs are quite buggy

and the butterflies are really beautiful and

the beetles are...

very silly.

The beetle gets stuck!
And his legs are very funny!

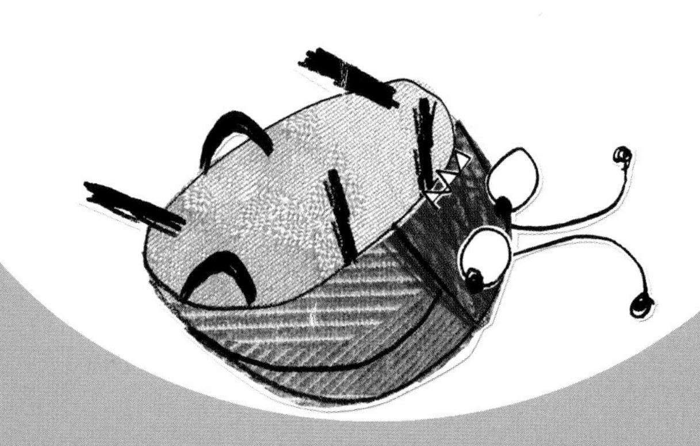

And he can't get down!"

I say,
"I know that, Lola.
Come on.
Dad's waiting."

"All his funny
little legs, Charlie!"

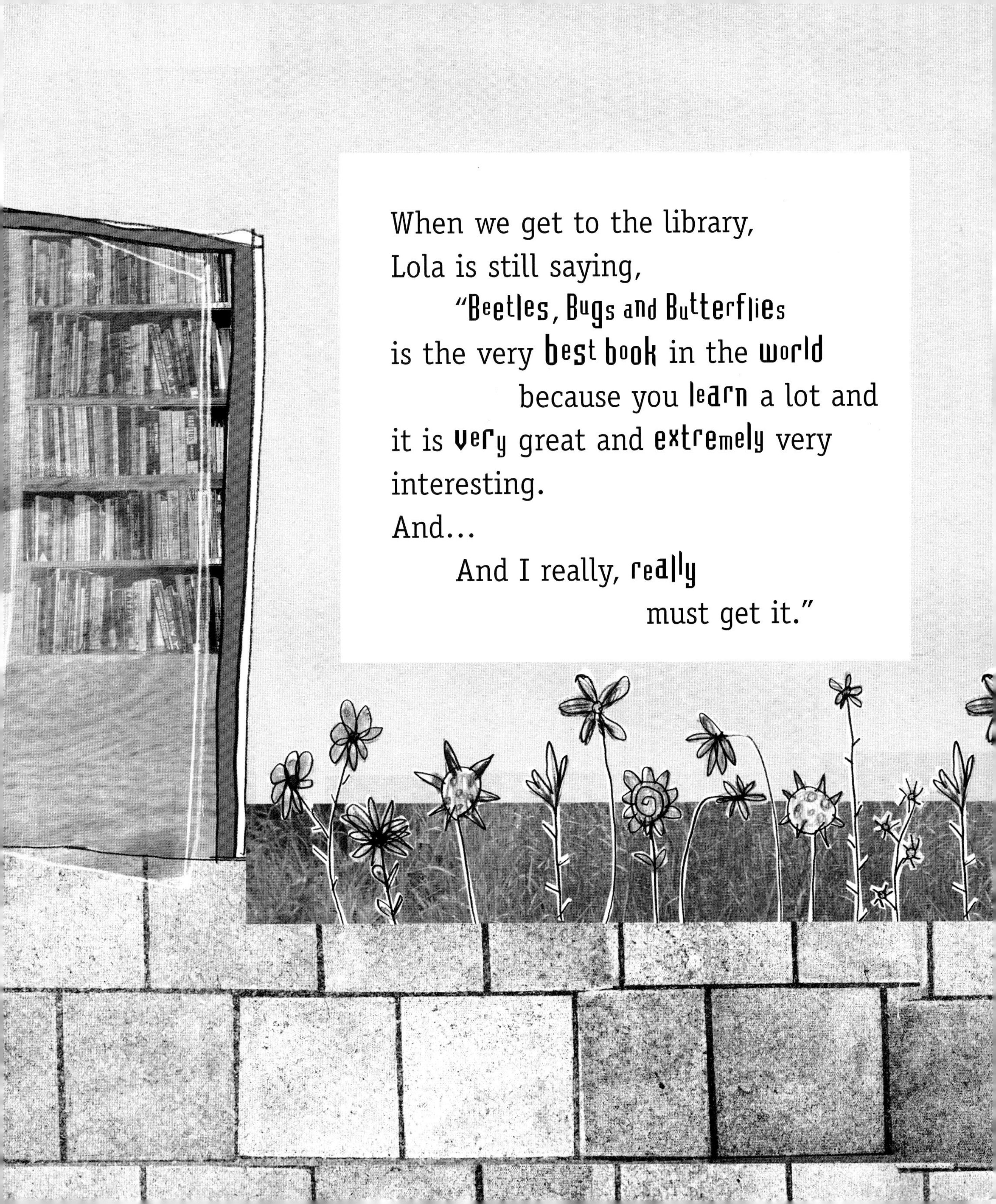

When we get to the library,
Lola is still saying,
"Beetles, Bugs and Butterflies
is the very best book in the world
because you learn a lot and
it is very great and extremely very
interesting.
And...
And I really, really
must get it."

Charlie

When we get inside
I have to say,

"Shh! Lola, it's a library.
We have to be quiet."

Lola says,
"But I can't find
my book, Charlie."

And I say,
"Then why don't you
try looking for it

with all the books
beginning with B?"

So Lola says,
"B, B, B... Where is my book?
Where can it be?"
I say, "Lola! Be quiet!"
She says,
"I am being quiet, Charlie!"
I say, "Shhhhh!"
She says, "I am shushing!
It's not there!
My book's not there!"

I say, "Lola! Be quiet!"
Lola says, "But Charlie, my book is lost!
It is completely not there!"

I say,
"Lola, remember this is a library
so someone must have borrowed it."

Lola says,
"But Beetles, Bugs
and Butterflies
is my book."

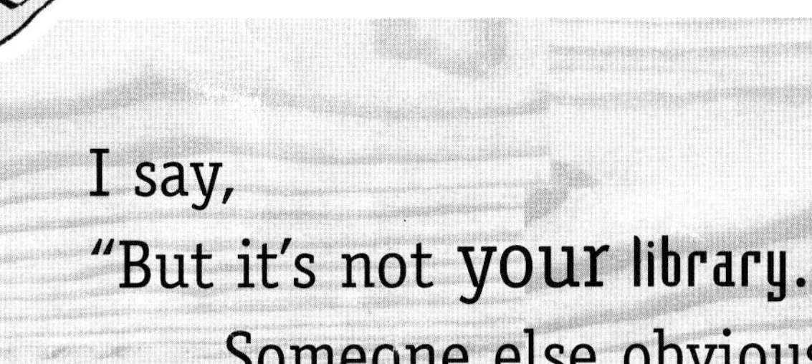

I say,
"But it's not your library.
Someone else obviously
wanted to read your book."

Lola says,
"But they can't. It's my book."

So I say, "Lola, just think.
There are hundreds and hundreds of other books
in the library to choose from.

There are spy books and dinosaur books. Adventure books

and scary books.

Books about princes,
aeroplanes and astronauts.

Books about castles,
dragons and volcanoes,

monsters,

mountains and pixies.

And books about Romans."

I say,
"Look! **Romans!** This one tells you
all about **history** in the **Roman times.**
Like how the **Romans** built long, straight roads
and rode chariots and had
fights with swords."

But Lola says,
"Too many
big
words,
Charlie.

ny book has got pictures that I really like.”
Romania
latinluk
retorom
Roma`li
rzymski
roma

So I say,
"OK, Lola, let's try to find
a book with more pictures and less words.

How about this? An encyclopedia?
It's got millions of drawings and millions of facts.
You can learn about **everything**.

Look, this page is all about helicopters."

"It's too loud, Charlie!
I don't really like encyclo...
ped... these big books.
Charlie
You see, Charlie, I am very right,
Beetles, Bugs and Butterflies
is the best book ever."

I say,
"You might be right, Lola,
but see what you
think of this...
It's a pop-up book."

But Lola says,
"A book that ha

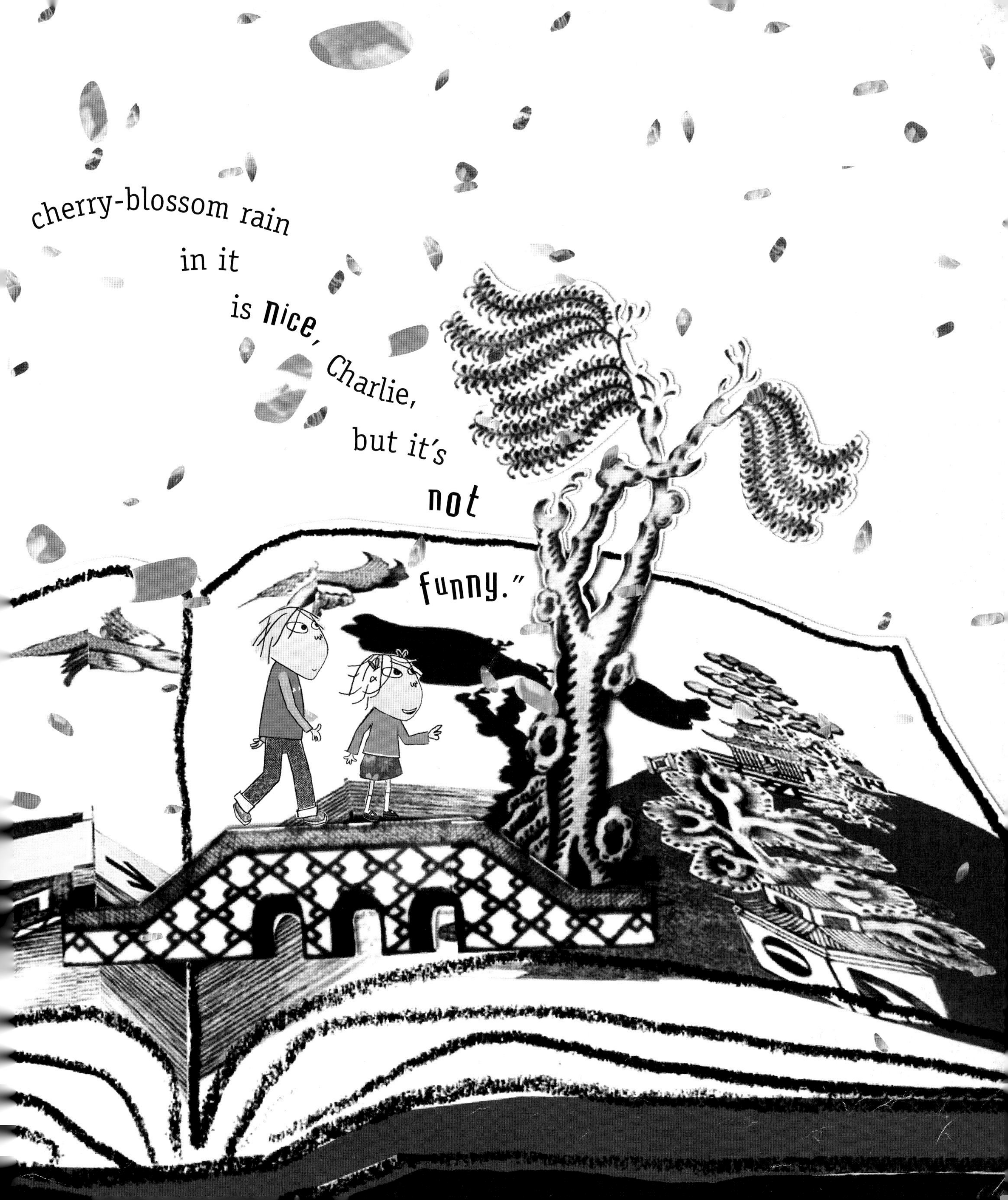
cherry-blossom rain
in it
is nice, Charlie,
but it's
not
funny."

Then Lola says,
"Beetles, Bugs and Butterflies
is really funny
and makes me
laugh

and

laugh

and

laugh..."

I say,
"So it's an **animal** book you want.
A book with... lots of pictures... a story...
no **big** words... and animals that make you laugh."
Lola says, "Yep."
I say, "How about **this**, Lola?! Cheetahs and Chimpanzees."
Lola says, "Are there
beetles, bugs and butterflies in it?!"
I say, "No, there are
cheetahs and chimpanzees.
Give it a try, Lola. Please."

Lola says, "OK, Charlie,
I will. But it won't
be as good as...

Beetles,

Bugs

and

Butterflies!

Oh no, Charlie! Look!

That girl's got **my** book!

I don't think she knows

it is

my book!

No, nOO...

Just wait...

That's **my**...

That's **my**...

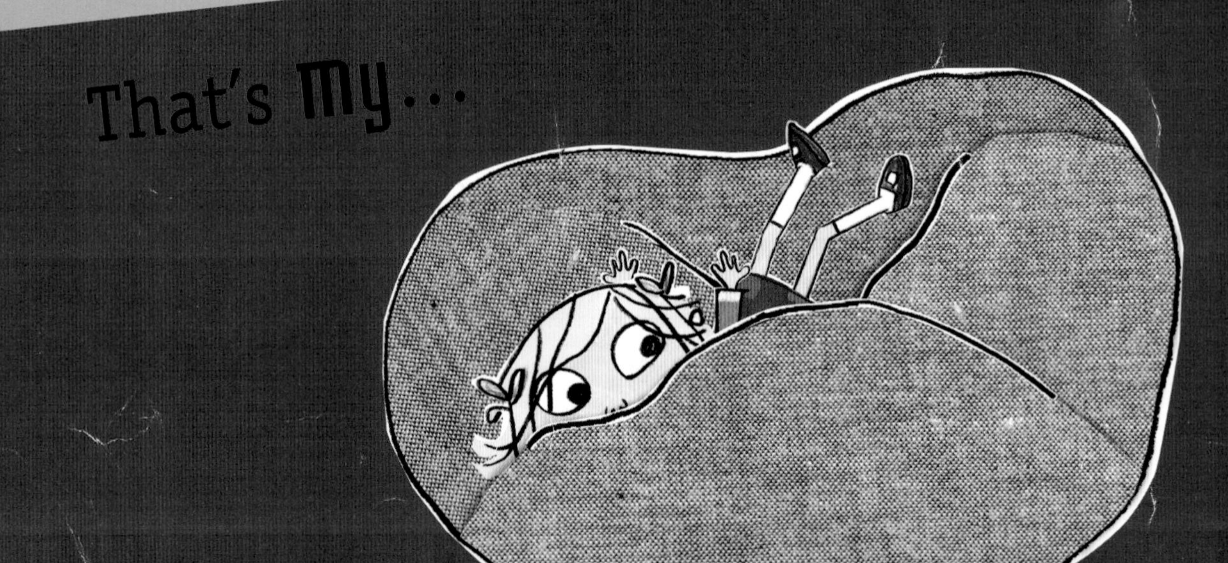

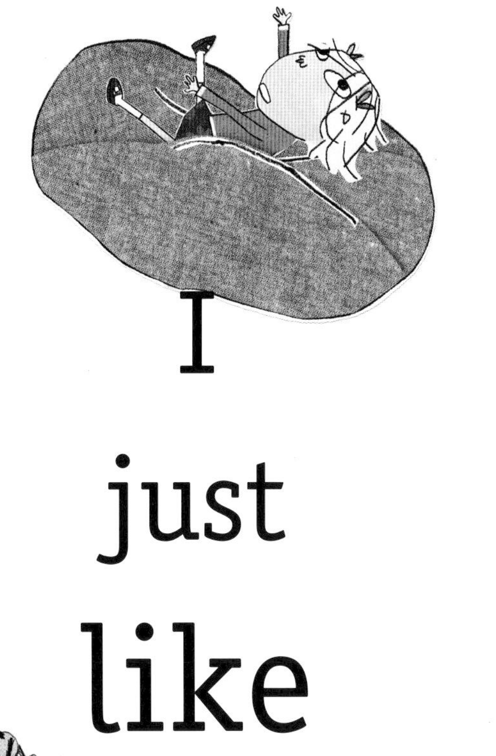

I just like my book, Charlie!"

OLIVER POSTGATE
Seeing Things
Children's Treasury of Milligan
IN THE EYE OF THE BEHOLDER
THE CHRISTMAS MYSTERY
Ardal O'Hanlon
miro
Lewis Wolpert
JEAN COCTEAU
ANIMAL STORYBOOK
The Faber Book of Contemporary Stories about Childhood
WILL SELF
The Quantity Theory of Insanity
Art and Artists
PRIMITIVISM AND MODERN ART
Sylvia Plath The Bell Jar
ch

Lola says,
"I want my book, Charlie!"
And I say,
"But you said you would try
Cheetahs and Chimpanzees."

Lola says,
"Well... I'll try it
but it won't be as good
as Beetles, Bugs and Butterflies."

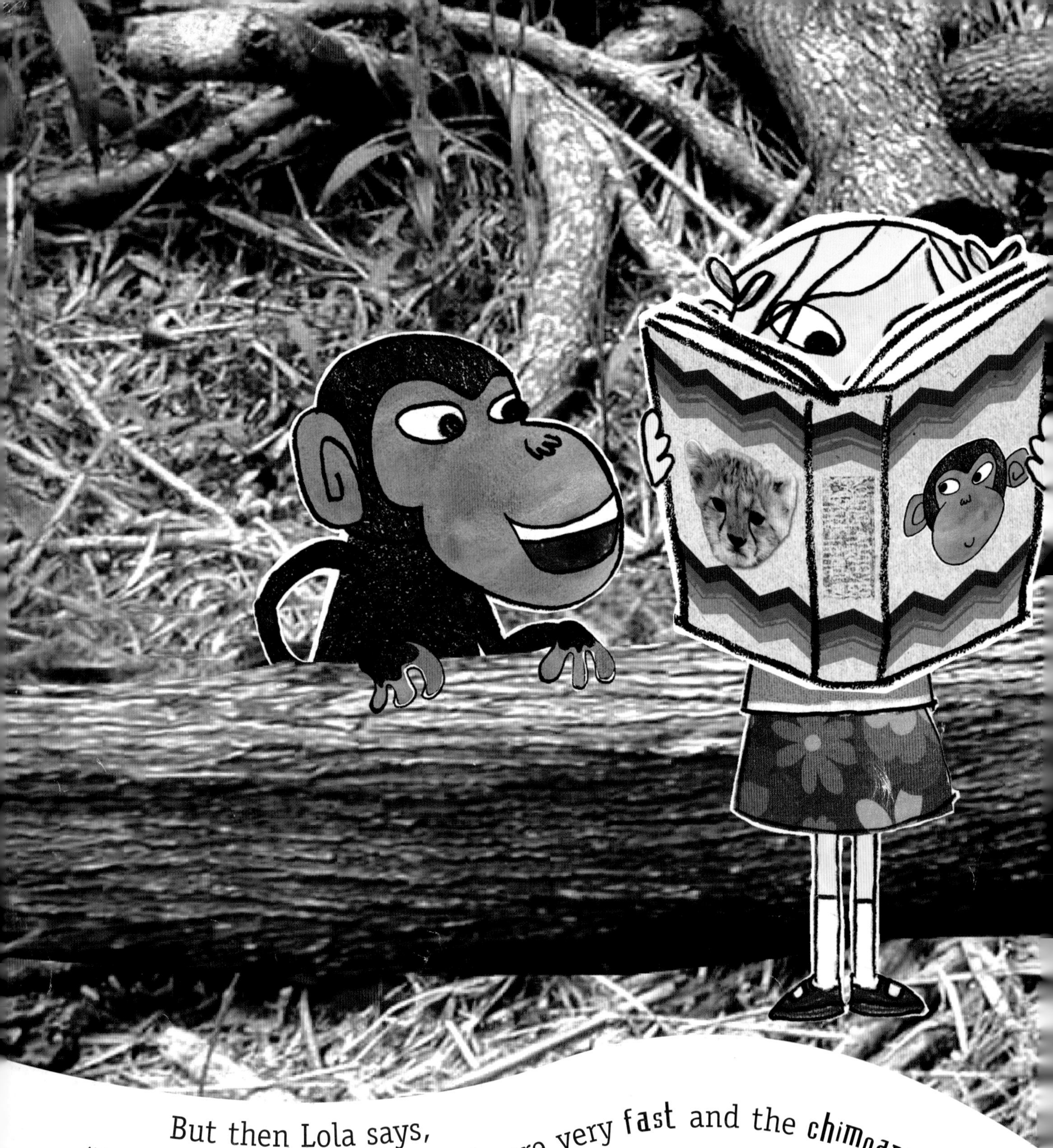

But then Lola says,
"Oh! Look at that. The cheetahs are very fast and the chimpanzees

are very cheeky and in fact, you know what, Charlie...?

This book is probably
the most best book in the whole wide world
because it is so interesting and so lovely
and you know it has the absolutely best pictures of any book ever
and the baby chimps are very funny..."